The Twisted Ending

Michael Ferguson

Published by Michael Ferguson, 2024.

While every precaution has been taken in the preparation of this book, the publisher assumes no responsibility for errors or omissions, or for damages resulting from the use of the information contained herein.

THE TWISTED ENDING

First edition. August 13, 2024.

ISBN: 979-8227205384

Written by Michael Ferguson.

Table of Contents

Chapter 1: New Beginnings

The move to Willow Creek felt like an escape, but Emily couldn't shake the feeling that they were running from something. The small town, nestled in a valley surrounded by thick forests, seemed like the perfect place for a fresh start. Yet, as Emily stared out the window of their moving van, watching the trees blur by, she couldn't help but feel an unease creeping into her chest. It was as though the towering pines were closing in on them, a green wall separating her from the life she once knew.

They pulled up to their new house—a modest, two-story home with peeling white paint and a sagging porch. It was a far cry from the bustling suburban neighbourhood they'd left behind, but it was all her mom could afford after the divorce. Emily's younger brother, Charlie, was already out of the van, running across the overgrown lawn, kicking up dead leaves as he went. Their mother stood by the front door, key in hand, a hopeful smile on her face. She looked tired, the dark circles under her eyes betraying the stress she tried so hard to hide.

"Isn't it charming?" her mom asked as Emily stepped out of the van, trying to sound upbeat. Emily forced a smile, but her stomach churned with anxiety.

"It's... something," Emily replied, trying to mask her disappointment. The house was old, much older than she had expected, with ivy creeping up the walls and windows that looked like they hadn't been cleaned in years.

Her mom shot her a quick look of concern before turning back to unlock the door. "It just needs a little TLC. We'll make it ours in no time."

As they stepped inside, the musty smell of dust and wood hit Emily's nose. The interior was dark, the sunlight barely penetrating through the heavy curtains that hung in the living room. The floorboards creaked underfoot, and Emily could hear the distant sound of Charlie running upstairs, his footsteps echoing through the house.

Emily wandered through the house in a daze, taking in the unfamiliar surroundings. The kitchen was small, with outdated appliances and faded wallpaper. The living room was cluttered with old furniture left behind by the previous owners, and the walls were lined with dusty bookshelves. Upstairs, the bedrooms were tiny, with low ceilings and windows that overlooked the forest. Her room was the smallest, just big enough for a bed and a desk. She dropped her backpack on the floor and collapsed onto the bed, staring up at the ceiling.

The silence was overwhelming. Back home, she'd been used to the constant hum of traffic, the distant sounds of neighbours going about their lives. Here, the only sound was the wind rustling through the trees outside. It felt like they were cut off from the world, isolated in this old, creaky house.

Emily's phone buzzed in her pocket, pulling her out of her thoughts. She pulled it out and saw a message from her best friend, Hailey, back in their old town.

Hailey: "How's the new place? Settling in?"

Emily stared at the message, her thumb hovering over the screen. How could she sum up the mix of emotions she was feeling? The loneliness, the fear of starting over, the resentment toward her parents for dragging her away from everything she knew. After a moment, she typed out a quick reply.

Emily: "It's okay. Just getting used to it."

She hesitated before sending it, feeling the emptiness of those words. But what else could she say? That she already hated it here, that the house felt like a prison, that she didn't want to face the prospect of a new school, new people, new everything? She sighed and hit send, knowing that nothing she could say would make her feel any better.

A few minutes later, her mom called up the stairs, breaking the silence. "Emily, Charlie! Come help with the boxes!"

Emily groaned and dragged herself off the bed. She trudged downstairs, where her mom was struggling to carry a box into the living room.

"Here, let me help," Emily said, taking the box from her. It was heavy, filled with books and picture frames wrapped in newspaper.

"Thanks, sweetie," her mom said, smiling weakly. "I know this move is hard for you. It's hard for all of us. But I promise things will get better."

Emily nodded, not trusting herself to speak. Her mom meant well, but it didn't change the fact that Emily felt like she was being uprooted from her life and planted in a place where she didn't belong.

They spent the rest of the afternoon unpacking, trying to make the house feel like home. By the time the sun began to set, they had managed to clear most of the boxes from the living room and set up the basics in the kitchen. They ate a quick dinner of takeout pizza on the floor, surrounded by boxes and paper plates.

After dinner, Emily headed back upstairs to her room, eager to escape the oppressive atmosphere of the house. She sat down at her desk and opened her laptop, hoping to distract herself with some videos or social media. But the internet connection was spotty, and her laptop struggled to load anything.

Frustrated, she closed the laptop and leaned back in her chair, staring out the window. The forest outside was dark and ominous, the trees casting long shadows across the yard. She shivered, feeling a chill run down her spine. The house was so isolated, so far from everything she knew. It was as if they were on a different planet, cut off from civilization.

Suddenly, she had an idea. Maybe if she made a TikTok video about the move, it would help her feel more connected to her old life. She grabbed her phone and started filming, showing off the old, creepy house and talking about how strange it felt to be in a new place.

"Hey, guys! So, this is my new house... as you can see, it's a bit of a fixer-upper," she said, turning the camera around to show the peeling wallpaper and dusty floorboards. "I'm not sure how I feel about it yet, but I'm trying to stay positive. At least there's a lot of... character?"

She laughed awkwardly and finished the video with a quick tour of her room, making jokes about the tiny space and the outdated decor. When she was done, she edited the video, added some music, and posted it to her TikTok account. It wasn't much, but it made her feel a little better, like she was reaching out to her old friends, even if they were miles away.

As she lay in bed that night, staring up at the ceiling, Emily couldn't shake the feeling of unease that had settled in her chest. The house was too quiet, too dark, too... lonely. She missed the noise, the energy of her old life. Here, everything felt muted, like she was trapped in a dream she couldn't wake up from.

She tossed and turned, unable to sleep. The wind outside howled, making the old windows rattle. Every creak and groan of the house set her nerves on edge. She tried to tell herself it was just the house settling, but the oppressive silence only made her anxiety worse.

Finally, she grabbed her phone and scrolled through TikTok, hoping to distract herself. She saw that her video had already gotten a few likes and comments from her friends back home, which made her smile. But as she scrolled through the comments, one in particular caught her eye.

Anonymous: "You shouldn't have moved here. Bad things happen in Willow Creek."

A chill ran down Emily's spine as she stared at the comment. Was it just a joke, or was someone trying to mess with her? She couldn't tell. She clicked on the user's profile, but it was blank—no posts, no followers, nothing. Just a username that gave no hints about who they were.

She shook her head and put her phone down, telling herself it was just someone trying to scare her. But the comment lingered in her mind, making it even harder to fall asleep. As she finally drifted off, the words echoed in her head, a dark omen hanging over her new beginning.

The next morning, Emily awoke to the sound of her alarm blaring in her ear. She groaned, her hand fumbling to silence it as she squinted at the time—7:00 AM. The first day at a new school. The thought made her stomach turn. She'd been up half the night, her mind racing with anxiety over the anonymous comment on her TikTok video. She tried to shake it off, telling herself it was nothing, but the unease lingered.

She dragged herself out of bed and stared at her reflection in the small mirror above her dresser. Her brown hair was a tangled mess, and dark circles had formed under her eyes. She looked as exhausted as she felt. After a quick shower, she threw on a pair of jeans and a hoodie, not wanting to draw any more attention to herself than necessary. The last thing she needed was to stand out on her first day.

Downstairs, her mom was already up, packing lunches for her and Charlie. "Good morning, sweetie!" she said with a forced cheerfulness that Emily could see right through. "Are you excited for your first day?"

"Thrilled," Emily mumbled, grabbing a piece of toast from the counter.

Her mom's smile faltered for a moment before she continued, "It's going to be great. New people, new experiences... you'll see. And I'm sure you'll make friends in no time."

Emily didn't respond, focusing on her breakfast instead. She could feel her mom's eyes on her, but she couldn't muster the energy to pretend she was looking forward to today.

A few minutes later, Charlie bounded down the stairs, his backpack slung over one shoulder. "I can't wait to check out the new school!" he said, his excitement the complete opposite of Emily's dread.

"Good for you," Emily muttered, stuffing the rest of her toast in her mouth. She grabbed her own backpack and headed for the door, not wanting to prolong the awkward morning any longer.

The walk to Willow Creek High was short, but the closer they got, the more Emily's anxiety built. The school was a small, red-brick building surrounded by tall trees, with a wide lawn out front. A few students were already milling around outside, talking in groups or scrolling through their phones. Emily took a deep breath and kept her head down as she and Charlie made their way inside.

As soon as they entered, the noise of a bustling hallway hit them. Students were moving from locker to locker, chatting and laughing, the sound echoing off the tiled floors and high ceilings. Emily felt like she was suffocating in the chaos. She clutched the strap of her backpack tightly, her knuckles turning white as she navigated through the crowd.

She found her locker and fumbled with the combination, her hands shaking slightly. When she finally managed to open it, she stuffed her bag inside and grabbed her schedule, scanning it quickly. First period was English, Room 204. At least it wasn't math. Math was always the worst on a first day.

With her schedule in hand, Emily hurried to Room 204, slipping into a desk at the back just as the bell rang. The classroom was small and cramped, with rows of old wooden desks and a chalkboard that looked like it hadn't been used in years. The teacher, a middle-aged woman with a severe bun, stood at the front of the room, droning on about the syllabus.

Emily tried to focus, but her mind kept drifting back to the comment on her TikTok video. Who would have written something like that? And why? She didn't know anyone in Willow Creek yet, so it couldn't have been a joke from a friend. The more she thought about it, the more uneasy she felt.

Halfway through the class, Emily's phone buzzed in her pocket. She glanced around to make sure the teacher wasn't looking, then quickly checked the notification. It was another comment on her video.

Anonymous: "You should really be careful in that house. Bad things have happened there."

Her heart skipped a beat. Was this the same person as before? How did they know about the house? Her hands trembled as she locked her phone and shoved it back into her pocket, her mind racing. Who was doing this? And why were they targeting her?

She tried to push the thoughts away and focus on the lesson, but it was no use. The rest of the class passed in a blur, the teacher's voice fading into the background as Emily's mind spiraled into worry. When the bell finally rang, she gathered her things in a daze and headed to her next class, barely aware of her surroundings.

By the time lunch rolled around, Emily felt like she was on the verge of a breakdown. She found a table in the far corner of the cafeteria and sat down, her appetite gone. She stared at her phone, half-expecting another notification to pop up, but the screen remained blank.

She was so lost in thought that she didn't notice the girl approaching her table until she spoke. "Hey, mind if I sit here?"

Emily looked up, startled. The girl was about her age, with blonde hair pulled back into a ponytail and bright blue eyes. She wore a friendly smile, but there was something sharp in her gaze, something that made Emily uneasy.

"Uh, sure," Emily said, forcing a smile.

The girl sat down across from her, setting her tray on the table. "I'm Megan. You're new here, right?"

"Yeah, I'm Emily," she replied, trying to sound normal despite the anxiety twisting in her gut.

"Welcome to Willow Creek," Megan said, her smile never faltering. "It's not the most exciting place in the world, but it has its charms."

"Thanks," Emily said, unsure of what else to say. She glanced around the cafeteria, noticing that several students were looking in their direction, whispering to each other. It made her feel even more self-conscious.

Megan seemed to notice too, because she leaned in and said, "Don't worry about them. New people always get attention around here. It'll die down soon enough."

Emily nodded, but she couldn't shake the feeling that something was off. Megan's friendliness seemed genuine, but there was an edge to it, like she was holding something back.

"So, how are you liking it so far?" Megan asked, taking a bite of her sandwich.

"It's... different," Emily said, struggling to find the right words. "The house we moved into is kind of old and creepy, but my mom says we'll fix it up."

"Oh, you moved into the old Montgomery place, right?" Megan asked, her tone casual, but her eyes were sharp.

"Yeah, how did you know?" Emily asked, her heart starting to race again.

"It's a small town. Everyone knows everything about everyone," Megan said with a shrug. "But you're brave to move in there. Most people wouldn't touch that place with a ten-foot pole."

"Why not?" Emily asked, trying to keep her voice steady.

Megan hesitated for a moment, then said, "There are rumours, you know? About what happened there. But it's probably just talk."

"What kind of rumours?" Emily pressed, her anxiety spiking.

Megan leaned in closer, her voice dropping to a whisper. "They say the house is cursed. That bad things happen to anyone who lives there. But it's probably just old superstitions. You know how small towns are."

Emily felt a chill run down her spine. Was this what the anonymous commenter was talking about? She tried to play it off, forcing a laugh. "Well, I hope the curse doesn't get me."

Megan smiled, but it didn't reach her eyes. "I'm sure you'll be fine. Just be careful."

The conversation left Emily feeling more unsettled than ever. Megan seemed nice enough, but there was something about her that made Emily wary. She couldn't shake the feeling that Megan knew more than she was letting on.

The rest of the day passed in a blur of anxiety and paranoia. Emily couldn't stop thinking about the comments on her video and the things Megan had said. By the time the final bell rang, she was ready to crawl into bed and hide from the world.

As she made her way out of the school, she felt a tap on her shoulder. She turned around to see a boy about her age, with dark hair and a serious expression. "You're Emily, right?"

"Yeah," she said, her heart pounding. Was he another person here to warn her about the house?

"I'm Luke," he said, his tone serious. "I heard you're living in the old Montgomery place."

Emily nodded, feeling a sense of déjà vu. "Yeah, why?"

Luke hesitated, glancing around to make sure no one was listening. "You need to be careful. That house... it's not safe."

"What do you mean?" Emily asked, her anxiety spiking.

Luke looked her in the eye, his expression grim. "Bad things have happened there. People say it's cursed. I don't know if it's true, but... just be careful, okay?"

Emily's heart raced as she stared at Luke, trying to process what he was saying. Was this another warning? Who were these people, and why were they all so concerned about her living in that house?

"Thanks, I guess," she said, not knowing what else to say.

Luke nodded, his expression softening slightly. "If you ever need to talk… or if something weird happens, just let me know. I live a few blocks away."

"Okay," Emily said, feeling a strange mix of fear and relief. She wasn't sure if she could trust Luke, but at least he seemed to genuinely care.

As she walked home, the weight of the day's events settled heavily on her shoulders. She couldn't shake the feeling that something was deeply wrong. The comments on her video, the warnings from Megan and Luke—it all seemed too much to be coincidence.

When she finally arrived home, the house felt even more oppressive than before. The shadows seemed to grow longer, the silence even deeper. Emily felt a sense of dread settle over her as she climbed the stairs to her room, her mind racing with all that had happened.

She needed to talk to someone, but she didn't know who to trust. Her mom was too busy trying to make everything work, and her friends back home were miles away. She felt isolated and alone, trapped in a house that seemed determined to make her life a living hell.

As she lay in bed that night, she could hear the wind howling outside, the trees creaking and groaning. She pulled the blankets up to her chin, trying to block out the noises. But the fear and anxiety gnawed at her, making it impossible to sleep.

The day had been a whirlwind of new experiences and unsettling encounters, and Emily couldn't shake the feeling that things were only going to get worse. She had moved to Willow Creek in search of a fresh start, but all she had found was a new set of fears and anxieties.

The darkness of the room seemed to press in on her, and she felt a growing sense of hopelessness. She didn't know what awaited her in the days to come, but she was certain of one thing: her life in Willow Creek was far from the fresh start she had hoped for.

Chapter 2: The Rise to Popularity

Emily's phone buzzed incessantly as she walked into school the next morning, her nerves frayed from the previous day's stress. She fished it out of her pocket, her eyes widening as she saw the number of notifications. Her TikTok video, which had been a light-hearted joke, had somehow gone viral overnight.

She scrolled through the comments and likes, her heart racing with a mix of disbelief and excitement. The video showed her attempting a ridiculous dance routine, one that she had thought was purely for fun. Yet, it had struck a chord with thousands of people, and now everyone at Willow Creek High seemed to be talking about her.

Emily's newfound fame became evident the moment she stepped into the school hallway. Students who had previously ignored her now greeted her with enthusiastic waves and smiles. "Hey, Emily! Loved your video!" one girl called out. "You're hilarious!" another student shouted as he passed by.

Emily felt a surge of confidence. The attention was overwhelming, but it was also exhilarating. For the first time since moving to Willow Creek, she felt like she belonged. Her TikTok fame had transformed her from an anxious newcomer into the center of attention. She couldn't help but bask in the glow of her newfound popularity.

In her first class of the day, Emily found herself surrounded by curious classmates eager to know more about her. "So, how did you come up with that dance?" one student asked.

"It just came to me," Emily replied with a shrug, trying to play it cool. Inside, she was still trying to grasp the whirlwind of attention she was receiving. "Just having some fun."

By the end of the day, Emily had made several new friends, all eager to include her in their lunch table and group chats. She found herself being invited to join various activities and social events. It was a stark contrast to the loneliness she had felt the day before. Her phone continued to buzz with friend requests and messages, and she couldn't help but feel elated.

At lunch, Megan from the day before approached her with a friendly smile. "Hey, Emily! How's it going? I see you're the new sensation around here."

Emily smiled back, feeling a sense of relief at Megan's continued friendliness. "Yeah, it's crazy. I never expected it to blow up like this."

Megan's eyes sparkled with curiosity. "Well, you're definitely the talk of the school. Just be careful, okay? Sometimes, people can get a little weird about sudden fame."

Emily nodded, though she didn't fully grasp what Megan meant. For now, she was revelling in the positive attention. Her confidence grew with each passing moment, and she was determined to make the most of this unexpected opportunity.

As the days went on, Emily's popularity only increased. Her social media following skyrocketed, and she became a regular topic of conversation among her peers. She started receiving invitations to parties and events, and she couldn't believe how quickly her life had transformed.

However, with the rise in popularity came a new set of challenges. Emily found herself constantly in the spotlight, and the pressure to maintain her image began to weigh heavily on her. She felt the need to keep up with the expectations and continue delivering entertaining content for her followers.

Despite the excitement, Emily began to notice subtle shifts in her interactions. Some students were overly eager to befriend her, while others seemed to harbour a sense of jealousy or resentment. The lines between genuine friendships and opportunistic relationships started to blur.

One afternoon, as Emily was heading to her locker, she overheard a conversation between two students in the hallway. "Did you see Emily's latest post? It's like she's trying too hard to stay relevant."

"Yeah, I know," the other student replied. "She's definitely changed since she got all this attention. It's like she's not even the same person anymore."

Emily's heart sank as she listened to the conversation. It was the first time she had heard criticism about herself, and it stung. She tried to shake it off, telling herself that she couldn't please everyone, but the negative comments lingered in the back of her mind.

Later that day, as she scrolled through her social media feed, she noticed a growing number of comments that were less than flattering. Some were straightforward critiques, while others were veiled insults masked as jokes. The positivity she had experienced seemed to be slowly overshadowed by a growing undercurrent of negativity.

Emily tried to stay focused on the positive aspects of her newfound fame, but the negative comments started to take a toll on her. She found herself increasingly anxious about maintaining her image and keeping up with the expectations of her followers.

As she lay in bed that night, she couldn't help but think about the people who had been friendly to her just a few days ago. Were their intentions genuine, or were they just interested in the hype? The thought made her uneasy, and she wondered if the sudden rise to popularity had brought with it an unforeseen set of complications.

Despite the growing unease, Emily continued to embrace her role as the school's new sensation. She attended parties, participated in school events, and kept up with her social media presence. The thrill of being in the spotlight was undeniable, but the pressure to maintain it was beginning to cast a shadow over her enjoyment.

As the week progressed, Emily's popularity showed no signs of waning. Her video had become a symbol of her success, but the increasing scrutiny and expectations began to take their toll. She knew that the rise to fame was not without its challenges, and she was determined to navigate them as best as she could.

The thrill of newfound popularity was beginning to wear off as Emily faced the reality of maintaining her social media presence. Her TikTok video had catapulted her to stardom, but the constant need to stay relevant was starting to feel like a heavy burden. What once felt exhilarating now seemed like a never-ending cycle of content creation and public scrutiny.

Emily's mornings were consumed by a routine of checking her social media accounts, responding to messages, and planning her next post. She was determined to keep up with the high expectations of her followers, but the pressure was beginning to overwhelm her. She found herself constantly thinking about what to post next, trying to balance authenticity with the desire to maintain her popularity.

One afternoon, during lunch, Emily sat at her usual table with Megan and a few new friends she had made. As she chatted with them, her phone buzzed with notifications. She glanced at it and saw that her latest post had received a surge of comments and likes. She forced a smile, trying to hide her mounting anxiety.

Megan noticed the change in Emily's demeanour. "Hey, are you okay? You seem a bit off today."

Emily hesitated, then forced a laugh. "Oh, I'm fine. Just a bit overwhelmed with all the social media stuff, you know?"

Megan nodded sympathetically. "I get it. It can be a lot to handle. Just remember to take care of yourself, okay?"

Emily appreciated Megan's concern, but she couldn't shake the feeling that she was becoming a puppet to her own fame. The pressure to keep her audience engaged was intense, and she found herself constantly seeking validation through likes and comments.

As the days went by, the demands of fame began to encroach on Emily's personal life. Her social media presence became all-consuming, and she struggled to find a balance between her online persona and her real-life interactions. She began to isolate herself from her family and old friends, dedicating almost all her time to maintaining her image.

One evening, as Emily was working on a new TikTok video, her mom knocked on her bedroom door. "Emily, dinner's ready. Do you want to come down and eat?"

Emily glanced at the clock and realized she had been working on her video for hours. "I'll be down in a minute," she called out, trying to hide her frustration. She was exhausted but felt compelled to keep pushing herself to stay relevant.

At the dinner table, Emily's family tried to engage her in conversation, but she was preoccupied with her phone. Her mom and dad exchanged worried glances as Emily's responses became increasingly curt.

"Is everything okay, sweetheart?" her mom asked gently.

Emily sighed, putting her phone down for a moment. "I'm just really busy with social media stuff. It's a lot to keep up with."

Her dad nodded, though he looked concerned. "Well, don't let it consume you. It's important to take breaks and enjoy time with us too."

Emily nodded, but the words didn't seem to sink in. She was too caught up in the pressure of maintaining her popularity to fully appreciate her family's concern.

As the weekend approached, Emily was invited to a series of parties and social events. Her calendar was filled with activities, and she felt a constant pressure to attend and be seen. The fear of missing out or appearing uninterested drove her to accept every invitation, even if it meant sacrificing her personal time.

At one party, Emily found herself surrounded by a group of admirers who eagerly sought her attention. They wanted to hear about her latest video, discuss trends, and take selfies with her. Emily put on a brave face and tried to enjoy herself, but inside, she felt a growing sense of exhaustion.

She caught a glimpse of Megan across the room, looking slightly uncomfortable as she observed the scene. Emily approached her, hoping for a moment of familiarity.

"Megan, hey," Emily said with a forced smile. "How's it going?"

Megan looked at her with concern. "I'm good, but I've noticed you've been really busy lately. Are you sure you're not overdoing it?"

Emily waved off the concern. "I'm fine. Just trying to keep up with everything. It's a lot, but I can handle it."

Megan's expression was a mix of worry and understanding. "Just remember, you don't have to do it all. It's okay to take a step back if you need to."

Emily nodded, but the weight of Megan's words felt heavy. The pressure to maintain her image was relentless, and she was struggling to find a moment of peace amidst the chaos.

That night, Emily lay in bed, her mind racing with thoughts about her online presence and the expectations that came with it. The thrill of being popular had given way to a constant state of anxiety. She felt trapped in a cycle of content creation, validation-seeking, and public scrutiny.

As she scrolled through her social media feed, she noticed that the positive comments were interspersed with increasing criticism. Some were from people who felt she was no longer genuine, while others criticized her for not living up to their expectations. The mixed feedback only added to her mounting stress.

Emily closed her eyes, trying to shut out the noise. She wanted to enjoy her success, but the pressure and scrutiny were starting to take a toll on her mental well-being. She longed for a moment of peace, but it seemed elusive amidst the demands of her new life.

Chapter 3: A Shadow in the Spotlight

Emily was starting to feel like she was getting a handle on her new life. Her social media following continued to grow, and she had made a comfortable niche for herself at school. Yet, the euphoric highs of her popularity were soon overshadowed by an unexpected and disturbing message.

It was a rainy Tuesday evening, and Emily was curled up in her room, scrolling through her phone. The storm outside provided a soothing backdrop as she relaxed, thinking about her next TikTok video. As she was about to switch apps, she noticed a new notification from an unknown account. The message was short and cryptic: "Watch your back. Not everyone is happy for you."

Emily's heart skipped a beat. She read the message several times, trying to decipher its meaning. It felt menacing, but she tried to brush it off. It could be from a troll or someone trying to get a rise out of her. Still, the ominous tone of the message lingered in her mind.

Her phone buzzed again, and she saw that her latest post had gone viral, but the earlier message had left her unsettled. Emily decided to share her concerns with Megan, hoping to get some perspective. She sent Megan a screenshot of the message and texted her: "Hey, just got this weird message. What do you think?"

Megan responded almost immediately. "That's creepy. Maybe it's just someone trying to scare you. Don't let it get to you."

Emily tried to take Megan's advice to heart, but the message continued to haunt her. She found herself constantly looking over her shoulder and feeling anxious about her surroundings. It didn't help that the message seemed to align with the growing negativity she had begun to notice online. Some comments on her posts had turned harsh and critical, but she had dismissed them as jealousy.

As the days passed, Emily's paranoia began to affect her daily life. She became increasingly wary of her classmates, wondering if any of them could be behind the anonymous message. Every interaction felt tinged with suspicion, and she found herself second-guessing people she had once considered friends.

One morning, as she walked to school, Emily noticed a group of students huddled together, whispering and glancing in her direction. Her heart raced as she tried to ignore them, but the feeling of being watched was inescapable. She hurried to her locker, hoping to find some solace in her familiar routine.

In the hallway, Emily ran into Sarah, a girl she had recently befriended. Sarah seemed unusually quiet and distant. Emily tried to make small talk, but Sarah's responses were curt and evasive. The awkwardness of the encounter left Emily feeling even more isolated.

Later that day, during lunch, Emily sat with Megan and a few other friends. She tried to focus on the conversation, but the earlier incident and the message from the anonymous account kept creeping into her thoughts. She felt disconnected, as if she were living in a world where everyone was just pretending to be friendly.

"Are you okay?" Megan asked, breaking the silence. "You've been really off lately."

Emily hesitated before responding. "I don't know. I've just been feeling really anxious lately. I got this weird message, and now I keep feeling like people are talking about me."

Megan's expression softened. "That sounds really tough. Maybe it's just your nerves. You've been under a lot of pressure lately."

Emily nodded, though she wasn't entirely convinced. She appreciated Megan's concern but couldn't shake the sense that something more sinister was at play.

That evening, Emily sat in her room, staring at her phone. The anonymous message had left her feeling vulnerable, and she couldn't help but wonder if the worst was yet to come. She tried to put her fears aside and focus on her next video, but the unsettling feeling lingered in the back of her mind.

As she worked, Emily noticed a new notification—a comment on one of her posts from someone with a suspicious username. The comment was vague but seemed to hint at knowledge about her private life. "Not everyone you meet is as nice as they seem. Watch your back."

Emily's hands trembled as she read the comment. It was as if someone was deliberately trying to unsettle her. She quickly deleted the comment and blocked the user, but the damage had been done. The sense of paranoia that had started with a single message was now becoming a pervasive anxiety.

With each passing day, Emily's sense of security eroded. She found herself constantly on edge, unable to relax even in the comfort of her own home. The anonymous attacks were starting to affect her mood and interactions, leaving her feeling isolated and distrustful of those around her.

The unsettling feeling that had plagued Emily was far from over. What started with a cryptic message had now escalated into a series of disturbing incidents. The line between her public persona and private life had begun to blur, and the attacks seemed to be intensifying.

It began with small, irritating disruptions. Emily noticed that her locker had been tampered with on several occasions. Her books and personal items were scattered or moved, though nothing seemed to be stolen. She brushed it off as typical teenage pranks, but the frequency and personal nature of these incidents began to erode her sense of safety.

The real turning point came when Emily's social media accounts were targeted. One evening, as she was preparing a new post, she discovered that her Instagram had been hacked. Photos were deleted, and her profile picture was replaced with a crude, mocking image. The hacker also posted inflammatory comments and personal details that Emily had only shared with a few trusted friends.

Panic set in as she tried to regain control of her account. She immediately contacted Instagram support and changed her passwords, but the damage had already been done. Her followers had seen the posts and the comments, and the negative attention spread quickly. Rumours and gossip fuelled by the hacker's actions began circulating throughout the school.

The following day at school, Emily's anxiety was palpable. She tried to act normal, but the stares and whispered conversations from her classmates made it clear that the hack had not gone unnoticed. The once friendly and welcoming atmosphere of Willow Creek High now felt hostile and judgmental.

During her lunch break, Emily sat with Megan and a few other friends. Megan was talking animatedly about an upcoming event, but Emily could barely focus. Her thoughts were consumed by the recent events.

"I can't believe someone would do something like this," Emily said, trying to sound casual but failing to hide her distress.

Megan glanced at her with concern. "It's really messed up. Are you okay?"

Emily forced a weak smile. "I'm just really shaken up. It feels like I can't trust anyone anymore."

Just then, another girl from their table, Jessica, spoke up. "Have you heard what people are saying about you? Some of the things that were posted were really harsh."

Emily's heart sank. She had hoped that people would understand the hacking was out of her control, but it seemed like the opposite was happening. The rumours and malicious comments had taken on a life of their own, and the situation was spiralling out of control.

Later that day, Emily received a message from a classmate, Tom, who she barely knew. "Hey, I saw what happened with your Instagram. That's messed up. If you need any help, let me know."

Emily appreciated the gesture but felt wary. She had no way of knowing whether Tom was genuinely sympathetic or if he had another agenda. The sense of mistrust was becoming a significant burden.

The tension continued to build as Emily's social media accounts faced further issues. Her Twitter was flooded with fake accounts and spam messages, and her Snapchat had been used to send out embarrassing images and false rumours. The attacks were relentless, and the personal and public humiliation was overwhelming.

Emily found herself increasingly isolated. She tried to confide in Megan, but their conversations were strained. Megan's own life was busy, and the constant drama surrounding Emily was starting to affect their friendship. Emily felt alone in her struggle and increasingly paranoid about her environment.

One afternoon, as Emily was leaving school, she noticed a group of students gathered near her car. They were laughing and pointing, and as she got closer, she realized they were looking at something on their phones. Emily's stomach churned with dread as she approached.

"What's going on?" she asked, trying to keep her voice steady.

One of the students, a girl named Lily, glanced at Emily with a smirk. "Just some interesting pictures of you. You should probably check your email."

Emily's heart pounded as she rushed to her car and pulled out her phone. There, in her inbox, was an email with a link. Hesitantly, she clicked it and was met with a collection of doctored photos and videos designed to humiliate her. The images were clearly manipulated, but they were convincing enough to stir up trouble.

Desperate to contain the damage, Emily contacted her parents and explained the situation. They were concerned but felt helpless. Emily's father offered to take action, but Emily was terrified of making things worse.

The emotional toll of the constant attacks was beginning to wear her down. She felt trapped in a nightmare where every attempt to fix the situation only seemed to make it worse. Her once confident demeanour was replaced by a constant sense of dread and vulnerability.

Chapter 4: Friendship on the Line

Emily's world, once vibrant and full of potential, was now shrouded in suspicion and paranoia. The relentless attacks from the anonymous hater had not only damaged her reputation but had also sown seeds of distrust among her circle of friends. The mounting pressure and personal nature of the sabotage made it increasingly difficult for Emily to distinguish between genuine support and deceit.

The once warm and supportive group of friends now seemed distant and uneasy. Emily's earlier attempts to lean on her friends for support had led to awkward exchanges and half-hearted reassurances. Her trust issues were becoming evident, and the strain was palpable in her interactions.

In the school cafeteria, Emily sat with Megan, Jessica, and a few others. She tried to join in on their conversation, but her mind was preoccupied with the latest harassment. Megan was discussing a new movie release, but Emily's focus was on the uneasy glances she received from Jessica.

"You know, I heard that someone was spreading rumours about you," Jessica said, her voice laced with a hint of bitterness. "Is there any truth to it?"

Emily's stomach churned. "No, it's all lies. I don't know why people are doing this, but it's getting really out of hand."

Megan tried to intervene, "Jessica, we should be supporting Emily, not questioning her."

Jessica's expression hardened. "I'm just saying, it's strange that all this is happening so suddenly. Maybe you should consider who you're really hanging out with."

Emily felt a pang of betrayal. "Are you saying you think I'm involved in this somehow?"

Jessica's face reddened. "No, that's not what I meant. It's just that everything seems so... complicated right now."

The conversation ended on a strained note, and Emily was left feeling more isolated than ever. She couldn't shake the feeling that Jessica's words were a reflection of a deeper mistrust that had begun to fester among her friends.

Later that day, Emily noticed Megan talking with some of the other students who had previously been part of her social circle. They were whispering and casting glances in Emily's direction. The sight stung, and Emily couldn't help but feel as though she was being ostracized.

Desperate to clear the air, Emily approached Megan after class. "Megan, is everything okay? It feels like something's changed between us."

Megan looked conflicted. "It's just that... with all the stuff happening, people are talking. And some of it doesn't paint you in the best light. I want to be supportive, but I'm also worried about the rumours."

Emily's frustration boiled over. "So, you're doubting me now too? I'm the one being attacked, and now you're questioning me?"

Megan's eyes widened with hurt. "No, Emily, that's not what I meant. I just don't know what to believe anymore. This whole situation is overwhelming for all of us."

Feeling a deep sense of betrayal, Emily walked away, her heart heavy with the realization that the support she once relied on was slipping through her fingers. The constant strain was driving a wedge between her and her friends, making her feel even more alone.

As Emily tried to navigate the treacherous waters of her social life, she began to question everything she had once taken for granted. The sense of security she once had was shattered, and the friends who had been her refuge now seemed like potential threats. The lines of trust had blurred, and Emily was left to grapple with a growing sense of isolation and distrust.

The growing rift between Emily and her friends set the stage for the next phase of her ordeal. As the attacks continued, Emily's isolation deepened, and the once-solid foundation of her social circle now felt fragile and unreliable. The emotional toll of the situation was evident, and Emily's struggle to maintain her friendships amidst the chaos became increasingly challenging.

The atmosphere at school grew increasingly tense as the days passed. Emily felt like she was walking on eggshells, trying to navigate the treacherous waters of her social life while grappling with the ever-present shadow of the anonymous attacks. The strain of the situation was starting to take its toll on her relationships, and the once-supportive friends now seemed to be drifting away.

One Friday afternoon, Emily and her friends had planned to work on a group project for their history class. The project was a chance for Emily to spend some time with her friends outside of the constant scrutiny, but the session quickly devolved into another painful confrontation.

As they gathered at Megan's house to work on the project, the atmosphere was charged with unspoken tension. Emily tried to focus on the task at hand, but the underlying discord was impossible to ignore. Jessica and Megan exchanged glances and whispered comments that Emily couldn't quite make out, but their demeanour spoke volumes.

During a break, Emily decided to address the elephant in the room. "Can we talk for a minute? I feel like there's something going on, and it's really affecting me."

Jessica sighed. "Emily, we need to be honest with you. The way things are going, it's hard for us to know what's real and what's not. People are talking, and it's becoming really difficult to handle."

Emily's heart sank. "So you think I'm faking this? That I'm somehow responsible for the drama?"

Megan jumped in, trying to mediate. "No one's saying that. It's just that everything's so mixed up right now. It's hard to trust anyone."

The frustration in Emily's voice was palpable. "I've been nothing but honest with you guys. I'm the one being targeted here, and now it feels like I'm being judged for it."

Jessica's expression hardened. "We're not judging you. But you have to understand that this situation is affecting us too. It's not easy to be caught in the middle."

Emily's eyes welled up with tears. "I thought you were my friends. I thought I could rely on you."

The conversation reached a breaking point, and Emily felt a sharp sting of betrayal as Jessica and Megan exchanged looks of exasperation. It became clear that the rift was too deep to bridge easily. The group project was abandoned, and the tension left Emily feeling more isolated than ever.

As she left Megan's house, Emily's thoughts were consumed with the sense of betrayal and the reality that her once-tight-knit group of friends was unraveling before her eyes. The feeling of being left out in the cold intensified, and she wondered if there was anyone she could truly trust.

The next day, the fallout from the confrontation became evident. Emily noticed that her former friends were now distancing themselves from her more visibly. The whispers and glances were more pronounced, and the once-friendly faces now seemed to carry an undercurrent of judgment.

Emily's social media presence, which had once been a source of validation, now felt like a double-edged sword. The viral fame that had propelled her into the spotlight was now a symbol of the deepening divide between her and those she had once considered close friends.

As the weeks wore on, Emily's isolation grew. The emotional toll of the attacks, combined with the erosion of her friendships, left her feeling vulnerable and alone. The support system she had once relied on had crumbled, leaving her to face the challenges of her social life and the relentless harassment on her own.

The fallout from the confrontation marked a turning point in Emily's struggle. With her friendships strained and her trust eroded, she was left to navigate the increasingly hostile environment with a growing sense of despair. The once-promising high school experience had become a battleground of mistrust and isolation, and Emily was forced to confront the harsh reality of her new social landscape.

Chapter 5: The Silent Enemy

Emily's days had become a haze of anxiety and fear. With her social circle in disarray and her trust in others eroded, she decided to take matters into her own hands. The attacks on her had escalated from mere nuisances to serious threats, and she felt a growing urgency to uncover the identity of her tormentor.

Armed with a notebook and a sense of determination, Emily began her investigation. She spent hours scrolling through her social media feeds, combing through comments, and tracking interactions that might provide clues. She scrutinized every post and message for any hint that might reveal the identity of the person behind the attacks.

Her first lead came from a series of anonymous messages that had taunted her for weeks. Emily noticed a pattern in the language and the timing of these messages. She began to suspect that the anonymous sender might be someone from her school, someone who had access to her social media and knew her personal details.

Emily decided to focus on her classmates, particularly those who had expressed hostility or jealousy toward her. She made a list of potential suspects, each with their own motives for wanting to see her downfall. She started with individuals who had seemed particularly sour during her rise to fame and worked her way through the list, trying to connect the dots.

She also revisited her encounters with various students, replaying conversations and interactions in her mind. Any seemingly innocuous remark or offhand comment was now scrutinized for hidden meaning. The process was exhausting and emotionally draining, but Emily pressed on, fuelled by a mixture of desperation and determination.

One evening, while going through a series of old messages and posts, Emily stumbled upon a suspicious exchange. A classmate named Olivia had left several comments on her posts that seemed innocuous at first glance, but Emily noticed a pattern. Olivia had been consistently commenting during the times when the anonymous attacks had intensified.

Emily's heart raced as she considered the possibility that Olivia might be involved. Olivia had always been somewhat on the fringes of Emily's social circle, never fully part of her inner group of friends. The more Emily thought about it, the more it made sense. Olivia's comments had often had a biting edge, and she had been noticeably absent from the group's recent interactions.

Determined to find out more, Emily decided to confront Olivia. She arranged to meet her in a quiet corner of the school library, hoping for a private conversation where she could probe without attracting attention.

When the day arrived, Emily felt a mix of nervousness and resolve. She approached Olivia, who was already seated at a table, flipping through a magazine.

"Hey Olivia," Emily said, trying to keep her voice steady. "Do you have a minute? I need to talk to you about something."

Olivia looked up, her expression shifting to one of curiosity. "Sure, what's up?"

Emily took a deep breath. "I've been getting some weird messages lately. I think someone from our school might be behind it. I noticed you've been commenting on my posts a lot, especially around the times when the messages started."

Olivia's eyes widened slightly, but she quickly masked her surprise with a nonchalant shrug. "I didn't think my comments would mean anything. I just thought they were funny."

Emily studied Olivia's face, looking for any sign of deceit. "Well, it's been really tough dealing with all this. I'm just trying to figure out who might be behind it."

Olivia seemed to consider her words carefully before responding. "I understand it's been rough for you, but I promise I'm not involved. If you want, I can help you figure out who's doing this. I wouldn't want anyone to go through what you're experiencing."

Emily hesitated, feeling a mixture of relief and skepticism. Olivia's offer seemed genuine, but the timing and context were suspicious. She decided to keep an open mind but remain cautious.

"Okay," Emily said. "I appreciate that. If you hear anything or see anything that might help, let me know."

As Emily left the library, she couldn't shake the feeling of uncertainty. Had she really found a clue, or was she simply grasping at straws? The investigation had only just begun, and the true identity of her tormentor remained elusive. For now, she was left to navigate the murky waters of suspicion and mistrust, hoping that her efforts would eventually lead to the truth.

Emily's attempt to unmask the person behind the attacks had left her on edge. Olivia's offer to help had seemed promising, but Emily was still plagued by doubt. She decided to follow up on her lead, hoping it would lead to some concrete answers.

For the next few days, Emily watched Olivia closely, analyzing her behaviour and interactions. Olivia was careful to act as though nothing had happened, but Emily noticed subtle changes. Olivia was more active on social media, commenting on posts and engaging in conversations with an intensity that seemed out of character. Emily wondered if Olivia was trying to cover her tracks or if it was just her imagination playing tricks.

Determined to confirm her suspicions, Emily gathered evidence of Olivia's online activity. She compiled screenshots of Olivia's comments and messages, trying to connect any dots that might indicate malicious intent. Despite her efforts, nothing concrete emerged, and Emily began to feel the weight of uncertainty bearing down on her.

One evening, as Emily was reviewing her notes, her phone buzzed with a new message. It was from an anonymous account, taunting her with a cryptic message: "Still looking, Emily? Maybe you should try closer to home." The message made Emily's heart race. It seemed like a direct challenge, and she wondered if her investigation had been discovered.

The message only fuelled her resolve. If Olivia wasn't the culprit, Emily needed to find out who was. She decided to escalate her investigation, reaching out to other classmates who had been distant or unfriendly. She hoped that by widening her net, she might uncover new leads.

Emily's search led her to another classmate, Mark, who had been known for his arrogance and frequent arguments with her. Mark had always seemed to resent Emily's sudden popularity. She decided to look into him more closely, studying his interactions and online presence.

To her surprise, Emily found a pattern in Mark's online behaviour that mirrored the anonymous attacks. He had posted derogatory comments about her on several forums and seemed to take pleasure in her misfortunes. Emily's initial excitement quickly turned to dread as she considered the possibility that Mark might be behind the attacks.

Determined to confront Mark, Emily arranged to meet him at a local café after school. She hoped that a face-to-face conversation might reveal more than a digital exchange. As she waited at the café, her anxiety mounted. Confrontations had never been her strong suit, and she feared that her accusations might be unfounded.

Mark arrived with a confident stride, his expression unreadable. Emily greeted him with a forced smile and led him to a secluded table. She took a deep breath and began, "Mark, thanks for meeting me. I need to talk to you about something important."

Mark's eyes narrowed slightly. "What's this about, Emily?"

Emily glanced around to ensure their conversation was private. "I've been getting some troubling messages and have noticed some patterns that lead me to believe you might know something about it."

Mark's demeanour shifted. He leaned back in his chair, his arms crossed defensively. "Why would I be involved in your drama? I'm not interested in your TikTok nonsense."

Emily felt a pang of frustration. "It's not just nonsense. These attacks are affecting my life, and I'm trying to find out who's behind them. I've seen some things that make me think you might be connected."

Mark's expression hardened. "If you're going to accuse me, you better have proof. I don't have time for this."

The tension between them was palpable. Emily's heart pounded as she tried to maintain her composure. "I'm not accusing you without reason. I just want to know if you've heard anything or if you know who might be behind this."

Mark's face was a mask of indifference. "I don't know anything. You're barking up the wrong tree."

Emily felt a wave of disappointment. The confrontation had not gone as planned, and she left the café feeling more confused than ever. The encounter with Mark had yielded no clear answers, only a deeper sense of frustration.

As Emily walked home, she replayed the conversation in her mind. Had she misjudged Mark, or was he simply good at hiding his true intentions? The lack of progress in her investigation was taking a toll on her morale.

When she arrived home, Emily tried to focus on her schoolwork, but her mind kept drifting back to the mystery of the attacks. The anonymous messages, Olivia's suspicious behavior, and Mark's defensive stance all seemed to point in different directions. She was no closer to uncovering the truth, and the stress was beginning to weigh heavily on her.

The next day at school, Emily's frustration turned into determination. She decided to take a different approach, hoping that a new strategy might yield better results. She planned to keep a low profile, observe her classmates more carefully, and look for any inconsistencies in their behaviour.

As Emily continued her quest for answers, she knew that each step forward might bring her closer to the truth or further into a web of deception. The search for the silent enemy had only just begun, and the path ahead was uncertain and fraught with challenges.

Chapter 6: The Downward Spiral

The relentless pressure from the attacks began to take a severe toll on Emily's mental and emotional well-being. What had once been a thrilling rise to popularity was now a nightmare of anxiety and self-doubt. She was no longer the confident, outgoing girl who had first arrived in Willow Creek; instead, she was a shadow of her former self, consumed by the torment of unseen enemies and the weight of her crumbling social life.

Emily's once vibrant presence on social media dwindled as she struggled to maintain the façade of normalcy. Her posts became erratic, reflecting the chaos of her mind. What had once been carefully curated content turned into a series of desperate, disjointed updates. Her followers, who had once eagerly awaited her next post, began to lose interest. The likes and comments that once fuelled her self-esteem now felt like a stark reminder of her growing isolation.

At school, Emily's performance faltered. Her grades, which had always been above average, began to plummet. She found it increasingly difficult to concentrate during classes, her thoughts constantly drifting to the latest attacks and the mounting pressure to uncover the identity of her tormentor. Teachers and classmates noticed her decline, but she brushed off their concerns with feigned smiles and vague explanations.

Emily's relationship with her family also began to suffer. She had always been close with her parents and younger brother, but now she kept them at arm's length. Dinners were tense, with Emily withdrawing into herself, barely participating in conversations. Her parents, worried about her sudden change in behaviour, tried to reach out, but Emily's responses were curt and dismissive. The once warm and supportive family environment had turned into a battleground of unspoken frustrations and hurt feelings.

Her room, once a sanctuary of creative expression, became a chaotic mess of discarded papers, half-written notes, and broken dreams. The once vibrant colours of her posters and decorations now seemed muted, mirroring her emotional state. Emily found solace in isolating herself in her room, avoiding any interaction that might remind her of her perceived failures and the relentless attacks.

Despite her best efforts to remain composed, Emily found herself increasingly haunted by paranoia. Every glance from a classmate, every whisper in the hallways, and every unfamiliar face seemed like a potential threat. She began to second-guess every interaction, convinced that everyone around her was either involved in the attacks or indifferent to her suffering. The walls of her once safe world were closing in, and the pressure was unbearable.

As the days wore on, Emily's attempts to hold on to some semblance of normalcy grew more desperate. She tried to maintain her old routines, but even simple tasks became monumental challenges. The weight of her declining grades, strained relationships, and fractured self-esteem became too much to bear. She felt like she was drowning in a sea of despair, with no visible lifeline in sight.

One night, as she lay in bed staring at the ceiling, Emily was overwhelmed by a sense of hopelessness. The attacks had escalated, and the anonymous messages had become increasingly cruel and threatening. She felt trapped in a cycle of fear and uncertainty, with no clear path forward. The weight of her social media fame, once a source of joy, now felt like a burden she could no longer carry.

In the midst of her emotional turmoil, Emily began to question her own sanity. She wondered if she was imagining the severity of the attacks or if her mental state had deteriorated to the point of delusion. The line between reality and paranoia became increasingly blurred, leaving her feeling disoriented and disconnected from the world around her.

The stress and isolation took a significant toll on Emily's mental health, leaving her on the brink of a complete breakdown. She felt like she was losing control of her life, and the sense of helplessness was suffocating. Her once bright future now seemed shrouded in darkness, and she struggled to find a way out of the downward spiral that had become her reality.

As Emily faced the mounting pressure and despair, she knew that something had to change. But with each passing day, the weight of her struggles became heavier, and the path to redemption seemed increasingly distant. The downward spiral had taken hold of her life, and Emily was left grappling with the consequences of her unraveling world.

The relentless strain of her deteriorating social status and the continuous harassment had begun to erode Emily's once bright and hopeful demeanour. Her grades, which had once been a point of pride, now suffered dramatically. Each test she took seemed to slip through her fingers, and her assignments, once meticulously completed, were now hastily thrown together. Teachers, who had previously praised her work ethic, now looked at her with a mix of concern and disappointment. The classroom had become a battleground where Emily fought not just to keep up with her work but to keep herself from collapsing entirely.

At home, the situation was no better. Emily had grown increasingly withdrawn, often shutting herself in her room for hours on end. Her parents, initially supportive and understanding, began to show signs of frustration. They worried about her isolation and were baffled by the change in their daughter's behaviour. Attempts to engage Emily in family activities or conversations were met with curt responses or complete silence. Her family could sense the deepening chasm but struggled to find a way to bridge it.

Emily's social media accounts, which had once been a source of validation and connection, now mirrored her internal chaos. Her posts became erratic—sometimes filled with desperate pleas for help, other times with angry rants or incoherent thoughts. The once supportive community online had turned into a battleground of harsh judgments and cruel comments. Each notification was a reminder of the growing disconnect between Emily and the world she had once felt so connected to.

The breaking point came one dreary afternoon. Emily had spent hours working on a project that, under normal circumstances, would have been straightforward. The stress of her worsening situation made the task seem insurmountable. She had been working on it all night, fuelled by a mix of anxiety and a desire to prove that she could still excel. As the deadline approached, she felt a mounting pressure that seemed to close in on her from all sides.

With just minutes left before the project was due, Emily's computer crashed. The screen went blank, and all her work vanished in an instant. Panic surged through her. She tried to restart the computer, but it remained unresponsive. Her hands shook as she frantically tried to salvage what was left, but it was clear that all her efforts were in vain.

In a moment of utter despair, Emily threw her computer across the room. The device crashed against the wall, its screen shattering into a mess of plastic and glass. The noise of the impact echoed through the empty room, mingling with Emily's sobs. She sank to the floor, her emotions spiralling out of control. The weight of her failures, the isolation, and the relentless attacks all seemed to come crashing down on her in that single, devastating moment.

Her parents, hearing the commotion, rushed into her room. The sight that met them was heartbreaking: Emily sitting amidst the wreckage of her computer, her face streaked with tears. They tried to comfort her, but their words seemed to fall on deaf ears. Emily was caught in a whirlwind of despair that seemed impenetrable, and she struggled to articulate the depth of her anguish.

The incident marked a profound shift in Emily's life. It was not just a failure of a school project; it symbolized a deeper collapse. The once vibrant and hopeful girl had been worn down by a relentless assault on her mental and emotional well-being. The breaking point was not merely a moment of crisis but a reflection of a broader, devastating loss of control.

As Emily sat in the aftermath of her breakdown, surrounded by the shattered remnants of her computer and the echoes of her cries, it became painfully clear that her path forward was uncertain and fraught with challenge. The fight to reclaim her sense of self and her place in the world seemed daunting, and the shadow of her silent enemy loomed larger than ever.

Chapter 7: The Final Blow

In the wake of her breakdown and the increasing isolation, Emily decided to make a drastic change. She felt that the only way to reclaim any semblance of control over her life was to cut off the source of her anguish entirely—her social media accounts. The decision was not made lightly. Each notification, comment, and message had become a tormenting reminder of her struggles. Her online presence, which had once been a symbol of her success, had now become a burden she could no longer bear.

The process of deleting her accounts was both liberating and terrifying. Emily went through each platform, erasing her profiles and posts, and shutting down her accounts one by one. As she clicked the final confirmation button, a wave of relief washed over her. The constant barrage of negativity was over, at least in the digital realm. But the relief was short-lived, as the reality of her decision set in. She was now disconnected from the world that had once given her a sense of belonging.

Emily's attempt to distance herself from everyone around her was equally intense. She stopped attending social events, avoided interactions with her remaining friends, and even began skipping classes. The isolation she had previously experienced in her room was now extended to all aspects of her life. Her parents noticed the drastic change but were unsure how to help. Their attempts to reach out were met with silence or curt responses, deepening their frustration and helplessness.

Despite her efforts to escape the turmoil, the world outside her digital bubble continued to spiral. Her absence from social media was noticed, and rumours began to swirl. People speculated about why she had disappeared and what might have driven her to such extremes. The gossip, while less immediate than the attacks she had faced online, was still a source of stress. Emily found herself haunted by the very things she had tried to leave behind.

In her quest for solace, Emily turned to old hobbies she had once enjoyed but had neglected in her pursuit of popularity. She began reading, drawing, and spending time outdoors. These activities, while providing a temporary escape, did little to address the underlying issues she faced. The loneliness that had initially driven her to seek validation online was now magnified by her self-imposed isolation.

Emily's mental health continued to deteriorate. She struggled with feelings of worthlessness and depression, and her physical health began to suffer as well. Her sleep patterns were irregular, and her eating habits became erratic. The once hopeful and vibrant girl was now a shell of her former self, grappling with the weight of her decisions and the consequences that followed.

The final blow came when Emily stumbled upon a message she had overlooked in her attempts to escape her digital life. It was an anonymous email, sent from an address she did not recognize. The message contained a single line that sent chills down her spine: "You can't hide from me forever." The realization that her efforts to escape had been in vain was crushing. The fear that the tormentor was still lurking, waiting for the right moment to strike again, overwhelmed her.

Emily's attempts to regain control had led to more than just personal turmoil; they had also led to a deepened sense of helplessness. The hater, who she thought she had left behind, seemed to be closing in on her once more. The isolation she had sought was now a prison, and the walls seemed to be closing in. In a world where every effort to reclaim her life only seemed to lead to further despair, Emily faced the stark reality that her battle was far from over.

Emily's attempt to disconnect from her online world and regain control of her life seemed to be working. With her social media accounts deleted and her isolation from her peers, she began to experience brief moments of peace. She focused on simple activities—reading, drawing, and spending time outdoors—trying to find solace and clarity.

But as weeks passed, Emily started to feel a growing sense of unease. Her previous fears, though suppressed, resurfaced with a new intensity. Despite her efforts to escape, she couldn't shake the nagging suspicion that someone was still watching her, lurking in the shadows.

One afternoon, while cleaning out her email inbox, Emily found a new message. It was an encrypted file with no subject line or sender information. Hesitant but driven by a mix of curiosity and fear, she opened it. The file contained a series of screenshots and messages from her former social media accounts—images of her most personal posts and private conversations, all of which had been collected before she deleted her accounts.

Among the files was a chilling video message. In it, a familiar face appeared—Lena, one of her former friends who had drifted away during the fallout. Lena, with a smirk on her face, spoke directly to Emily. "Thought you could hide from me, didn't you? You really thought you could just walk away and leave me behind? Well, it's not over. Not by a long shot."

The betrayal hit Emily like a punch to the gut. Lena had been one of her confidantes, someone she had trusted during the most tumultuous time. The revelation that Lena had been behind the attacks all along shattered Emily's remaining sense of security. Lena's motivations became painfully clear: jealousy and resentment. She had orchestrated the campaign of harassment to bring Emily down from her pedestal, driven by her own insecurities and grudges.

Feeling utterly defeated, Emily tried to confront Lena directly. She arranged a meeting, hoping for some semblance of closure or understanding. Lena met her at a local park, where they had shared many good times before the chaos. As Emily approached, Lena's demeanour was cold and detached, her earlier smirk replaced with a stoic expression.

"I should have known it was you," Emily said, her voice trembling with a mix of anger and sorrow. "Why, Lena? Why did you do this?"

Lena's response was dismissive. "You were always so full of yourself. I just wanted to show you that you're not as invincible as you thought. You've done nothing but flaunt your popularity and make everyone around you feel insignificant. I had to bring you down."

The confrontation quickly escalated. Lena's contempt and Emily's hurt collided, leading to a heated exchange. Their arguments grew louder, attracting the attention of passersby. Emily, feeling cornered and exposed, realized that Lena's cruelty was unrelenting. She had hoped for an explanation or an apology but was met with disdain and further mockery.

The public scene and the unresolved confrontation only added to Emily's distress. The exposure of Lena's role in the attacks became a new point of ridicule and gossip among their peers. Emily's attempt to confront her tormentor had backfired, leaving her reputation further damaged and her emotional state more fragile than ever.

As Emily walked away from the park, she felt the weight of her recent revelations settling heavily on her shoulders. Lena's betrayal had not only added a new layer of anguish but also deepened Emily's sense of isolation. She had sought answers and found only more pain. The trust she had once placed in others had been irrevocably broken, leaving her to grapple with the harsh reality of her situation.

Chapter 8: The Unraveling

Emily had hoped that confronting Lena would finally bring her the closure she desperately needed. Armed with the evidence of Lena's manipulation and deceit, she arrived at the park where they had met before. This time, she was resolute, determined to face her tormentor and force an explanation.

As she approached the park's central gazebo, Emily noticed Lena standing alone, waiting with an unreadable expression. Lena's casual stance and indifferent gaze made Emily's heart race with a mix of dread and resolve.

"I'm done playing games," Emily declared as she stepped closer. "I know it was you behind everything. Why did you do this to me?"

Lena's face remained emotionless as she replied, "You should have known better than to think you could just waltz into this town and become the center of attention without some backlash. You had it coming."

Emily's frustration flared. "This wasn't just about me. You've hurt so many people in the process. Why couldn't you just let it go?"

Lena's smirk returned. "Because watching you crumble was too tempting. I wanted you to experience the same insecurities and fears that I've dealt with."

The conversation quickly escalated as Lena's anger and Emily's desperation clashed. Lena began taunting Emily, mocking her attempts to regain control and highlighting every mistake Emily had made. Their argument grew louder, drawing the attention of nearby park-goers.

Emily tried to maintain her composure, but Lena's relentless attacks pushed her to the edge. Her frustration turned into tears as she pleaded with Lena to stop, to acknowledge the damage she had done. But Lena seemed unmoved by Emily's pleas.

As their confrontation reached a fever pitch, Lena's anger took a more dangerous turn. She started making threats, hinting at further consequences if Emily didn't back off. Emily realized too late that Lena's hostility was more than just verbal—it was a looming threat of escalating violence.

Feeling cornered and terrified, Emily attempted to leave, hoping to escape the volatile situation. But Lena blocked her path, refusing to let her go without a final confrontation. The scene was becoming increasingly chaotic, with bystanders watching in alarm as the two former friends faced off.

Emily's heart pounded as Lena's threats grew more explicit and menacing. The fear of physical confrontation and further humiliation overwhelmed her. She knew she needed to get away from Lena before things spiralled completely out of control.

In a desperate move, Emily pushed past Lena and ran towards the park's exit. Lena's angry shouts followed her, but Emily didn't look back. She fled the park, her mind racing with fear and anger. The confrontation had not only failed to provide the closure she sought but had also deepened her sense of vulnerability.

As Emily reached the safety of her home, she was left with a haunting realization. Lena's betrayal had not only ruined her social standing but had also exposed her to a dangerous level of hostility. The confrontation had shattered any remaining illusions of resolution and had only added to the mounting pressure and despair Emily felt.

The aftermath of Emily's confrontation with Lena was a whirlwind of chaos and devastation. The park incident had drawn widespread attention, and the details of their argument spread quickly through the school and local media. Despite Emily's hope for a resolution, the fallout was far worse than she had anticipated.

Emily's social media accounts, which she had briefly thought she could escape by deleting them, were inundated with comments and posts about the confrontation. Videos and photos from the park had been shared widely, turning her into a subject of mockery and scorn. The very platform that had once elevated her now became a battleground where she was ridiculed and vilified.

At school, the atmosphere was hostile. Emily's former friends avoided her, and even those who had previously shown support were now hesitant to associate with her. Gossip and speculation about the confrontation and Lena's motivations filled the hallways, further isolating Emily. Her attempts to clear the air or explain her side of the story were met with indifference or outright hostility.

Her family, once a source of strength, struggled to understand the full extent of the situation. They were shocked by the public's reaction and frustrated by Emily's inability to escape the chaos. Conversations at home grew tense, and Emily's isolation extended beyond school and social media into her own home.

The psychological impact of the public shaming and the betrayal weighed heavily on Emily. She found it increasingly difficult to distinguish between her actual friends and the numerous people who now seemed to delight in her downfall. The once-familiar environment of Willow Creek had transformed into a hostile and unwelcoming place.

Emily's attempts to salvage any remaining fragments of her reputation proved futile. The exposure of Lena's identity had done little to shift the blame away from her. If anything, it only intensified the scrutiny and criticism she faced. Lena's motives, while vindicated in their maliciousness, were overshadowed by the relentless cycle of blame and shame that Emily endured.

As Emily retreated further into her shell, she began to grapple with a profound sense of loss and betrayal. The emotional and social scars from the confrontation were deep, leaving her feeling disillusioned and hopeless. The promise of a fresh start in Willow Creek had turned into a relentless nightmare, and Emily's world seemed to unravel further with each passing day.

The chapter closes with Emily standing alone in her room, staring at the remnants of her once-thriving online presence now reduced to a series of negative comments and cruel memes. The isolation and despair that had enveloped her felt insurmountable, leaving her to ponder the future in a state of deepening darkness.

Chapter 9: The Collapse

Emily's life had become a shadow of what it once was. After the public confrontation and the subsequent fallout, she withdrew completely from the world around her. Her room, once a vibrant space filled with posters and bright colours, now felt like a prison. The walls seemed to close in as she sank deeper into isolation.

School had become a gauntlet of whispered judgments and sidelong glances. The once-familiar faces of classmates were now turned away, their expressions cold and distant. Teachers, once supportive, now looked upon her with a mixture of pity and disapproval. Emily's attempts to engage with her schoolwork faltered as her focus wavered and her grades plummeted.

At home, the atmosphere was strained. Her parents tried to reach out, but Emily's responses were curt and unenthusiastic. They watched helplessly as their daughter spiralled further into depression, their attempts to offer comfort met with resistance. Family dinners, once filled with laughter, became tense and awkward, overshadowed by Emily's growing silence.

Her social media presence, which had once been a source of validation, was now a reminder of her downfall. She had deactivated her accounts, but the residual effects of the harassment lingered. Old posts and screenshots circulated among her peers, fuelling ongoing harassment and making it impossible for her to escape the digital scars of her past.

Emily's only solace was the time she spent alone in her room, where she would sit for hours, lost in her thoughts. She avoided mirrors, unable to face the reflection of the person she had become. The isolation was complete, leaving her in a state of numbness as she struggled to come to terms with the reality of her situation.

Her once-hopeful outlook had given way to despair. The dreams of a bright future had vanished, replaced by a bleak sense of inevitability. Emily's world had shrunk to the confines of her room, and even the simplest tasks, like getting out of bed or eating, had become monumental challenges.

As the days passed, Emily's sense of self-worth continued to deteriorate. She felt like a ghost in her own life, disconnected from the world she had once been so actively a part of. The weight of her isolation was unbearable, leaving her in a state of profound sadness and resignation.

The walls of Emily's room, once a sanctuary from the outside world, had become a prison. Days blurred into one another, marked only by the occasional change of clothes and the dim light of her laptop, which she rarely used anymore. Her once vibrant social media accounts were now deactivated, and her only remaining connection to the world was through the barely audible hum of the outside traffic. The isolation was suffocating, and the weight of her own thoughts pressed heavily on her.

Emily's room was a mess—a stark contrast to her previous organized and vibrant space. Clothes were strewn across the floor, half-eaten takeout containers piled up on her desk, and unopened letters lay scattered on her bed. The once-cherished items that decorated her walls were now hidden under a veil of dust. Her mirror, which used to reflect her daily preparations, had become an ominous reminder of her descent.

Her parents, though well-meaning, had become increasingly concerned. They had tried everything—encouraging her to talk to a counsellor, engaging in family activities, and offering support. Yet, every attempt seemed to fall short. Their daughter had retreated into a shell, and no matter how much they reached out, they could not break through.

At school, Emily had become a ghost. The hallways that once buzzed with conversations now felt oppressive, each echo of laughter or conversation a reminder of her estrangement. Her teachers, who had been supportive, now looked at her with a mixture of pity and frustration. They had seen her decline and were at a loss for how to help. The once-engaged student who had participated in class and had a bright future ahead of her was now a shadow, barely keeping up with her assignments.

Emily's attempts to find solace in the outside world were futile. The weight of the hater's actions had shattered her confidence. The overwhelming sense of betrayal and public humiliation had led her to sever ties with everyone, including her remaining friends. The few who had tried to reach out were met with cold silence or, worse, hostile responses.

Her emotional state was precarious. The despair that had set in was all-consuming, leaving her unable to see a way out. She felt trapped in a cycle of negative thoughts, with no clear path to recovery. The occasional moments of clarity she experienced were overshadowed by a pervasive sense of hopelessness.

One particularly dark evening, Emily found herself sitting by her window, staring at the street below. The streetlights cast long shadows, and the world outside seemed to continue on as if her own turmoil was inconsequential. It was a stark contrast to the chaos in her mind. She had been grappling with thoughts of how her life had unraveled, questioning where it had all gone wrong. The isolation had reached a point where it was almost unbearable.

Emily's mind drifted back to the time when things had started to fall apart—the viral TikTok video, the swift rise to popularity, and the subsequent attacks. Each memory felt like a stab wound, reopening old wounds and intensifying her despair. She wondered if things could have been different, if she could have handled the pressure better, or if she had somehow invited the torment upon herself.

The idea of taking drastic action had crossed her mind before, but she had always managed to push it aside. Tonight, however, the thoughts seemed more persistent. The isolation, the guilt, and the feeling of being trapped were overwhelming. Emily's mind raced through different scenarios, trying to find an escape from the pain that had become her constant companion.

In a moment of profound desperation, Emily reached for her phone. It had been lying untouched on her bedside table, a relic of a time when she had been connected to the world. She scrolled through old messages and notifications, each one a reminder of what her life had once been and what it had become. The thought of reaching out for help seemed futile, as she felt no one could truly understand the depth of her anguish.

As the night deepened, Emily's thoughts became darker. She felt a strange sense of calm as she considered the idea of escape. It wasn't a decision made lightly, but rather a culmination of the endless days of despair and isolation. The idea of ending the pain seemed almost like a release, a way to escape from the relentless cycle of torment and sadness.

Emily's parents, unaware of the full extent of her internal struggle, were in their own world of worry. They had noticed the signs—Emily's withdrawal, her declining grades, and the uncharacteristic silence. They had sought help from counsellors and professionals, but Emily's refusal to engage with them made the process slow and challenging. They had hoped that time would heal the wounds, but as the days turned into weeks, their hope began to wane.

The crisis point came unexpectedly. It was a moment of profound darkness, where Emily felt she could no longer bear the weight of her circumstances. The decision she made that night was a reflection of her state of mind—a culmination of her feelings of hopelessness and despair.

The next morning, her parents found the aftermath of Emily's desperation. The discovery was shocking and heartbreaking, a moment that would forever alter their lives. They were faced with the devastating reality of their daughter's plight, and the knowledge that they had not been able to prevent it was almost too much to bear.

The news of Emily's drastic decision spread quickly through the community. The response was a mix of shock, sympathy, and regret. Many people who had been quick to judge Emily during her rise and fall now found themselves reflecting on the consequences of their actions and the role they had played in her suffering. The realization that Emily's isolation had led her to such a desperate place was a sobering reminder of the impact of public scrutiny and personal betrayal.

In the aftermath, Emily's story became a cautionary tale—a stark reminder of the fragility of mental health and the importance of empathy and support. The community was left to grapple with the fallout, and Emily's parents faced the difficult task of coming to terms with their loss while trying to understand how things had gone so terribly wrong.

The collapse of Emily's world had been sudden and tragic, a reflection of the profound impact that social media, public judgment, and personal betrayal could have on an individual's mental health. Her story served as a painful reminder of the need for compassion and understanding in a world that often failed to provide either.

Chapter 10: The Haunting Truth

The days following Emily's drastic decision were shrouded in a heavy silence. Her parents were devastated, unable to fully process the enormity of what had transpired. The once bustling household was now characterized by an eerie stillness, with every corner of the house echoing the absence of Emily's vibrant presence. They were in shock, struggling to come to terms with the reality of their daughter's situation.

Emily, meanwhile, was isolated in a hospital room, her mind a tumult of confusion and despair. The attempt on her life had been a cry for help, a desperate bid to escape the unbearable weight of her circumstances. As she lay there, she was confronted with the gravity of her actions and the ramifications they would have on her future. The emotional and psychological toll was immense, and she found herself grappling with a profound sense of guilt and regret.

It was during this time of enforced reflection that Emily began to uncover the disturbing truths about her tormentor. Her parents, having been contacted by the authorities, were informed that Emily's case was being investigated. They were assured that efforts were being made to uncover the identity of the hater who had caused so much pain. For Emily, this news was a bittersweet comfort—on one hand, it meant that someone might be held accountable, but on the other, it reopened old wounds and stirred up new fears.

The investigation led Emily's parents to uncover information that had previously been hidden from them. They discovered that the harassment Emily had endured was not random or baseless but rather driven by deeply personal motivations. As the details emerged, it became clear that the hater's actions were fuelled by a troubled past and a personal vendetta.

Emily, though still recovering physically and emotionally, was determined to find out more about her tormentor. With the support of her family and under the guidance of her therapist, she began to piece together the puzzle of her tormentor's identity. The revelations were shocking and unsettling.

The hater, it turned out, was someone from Emily's own school—a student who had been quietly harbouring resentment and jealousy. This individual had been envious of Emily's sudden rise to fame and had used their access to her social media accounts to orchestrate the campaign of harassment. The motivation behind the attacks was not merely a desire for revenge but also a deep-seated need for control and power.

Emily's investigation revealed that the hater had a history of being bullied and ostracized, which had contributed to their toxic mindset. The hater had projected their own insecurities and frustrations onto Emily, using her as a scapegoat for their unresolved issues. The more Emily learned, the clearer it became that the hater's actions were a reflection of their own pain and suffering, rather than a direct attack on her personal character.

The disturbing truth about the hater's motivations left Emily reeling. She had been the target of a campaign that was as much about the hater's internal struggles as it was about her own perceived faults. The realization that her suffering had been intertwined with someone else's deep-seated issues was both sobering and painful.

Emily's parents were also confronted with the harsh reality of the situation. They had initially struggled to understand how such an intense and personal attack could have happened to their daughter. The investigation shed light on the broader issues of bullying, mental health, and the impact of social media on young people's lives. It became clear that the hater's actions were not an isolated incident but part of a larger pattern of behaviour that needed to be addressed.

As Emily began to process these revelations, she faced a tumult of emotions. The knowledge that her tormentor had been driven by personal pain did not necessarily alleviate her own suffering, but it provided a context that helped her understand the situation better. The hater's motivations, while deeply troubling, also offered a glimmer of insight into the broader issues at play.

The truth about the hater was revealed to the public, adding another layer to Emily's already complex situation. The community was shocked to learn about the personal struggles and motivations behind the attacks. Many people who had previously been quick to judge Emily's actions and reactions now found themselves reconsidering their perspectives. The revelation led to a wave of sympathy for Emily but also sparked discussions about the need for greater awareness and support for mental health issues among young people.

For Emily, the revelations were a double-edged sword. On one hand, understanding the hater's motivations provided some measure of closure and context. On the other hand, it also deepened her sense of betrayal and hurt. The emotional and psychological scars left by the campaign of harassment were not easily healed, and the process of coming to terms with the truth was fraught with difficulty.

In the aftermath of the revelations, Emily's journey towards recovery was just beginning. The truth about the hater's motivations offered a new perspective, but it also highlighted the need for continued support and healing. Emily, with the help of her family and therapist, began to confront the emotional and psychological toll of her experiences, working towards a future where she could find peace and reclaim her sense of self.

The haunting truth about the hater's motivations was a crucial piece of the puzzle, providing a deeper understanding of the forces at play. However, it was also a reminder of the complex and multifaceted nature of human behaviour and the impact that personal struggles can have on others. For Emily, the path ahead was uncertain, but the revelations marked a critical step in her journey towards healing and self-discovery.

Emily lay on her bed, staring at the ceiling, her mind racing with the weight of her recent revelations. The hospital room had become her refuge, a place where she could momentarily escape from the turmoil of the outside world. But even within these sterile walls, she was not free from the consequences of her actions and the impact of the hater's manipulations.

The truth about the hater's motivations had provided some clarity, but it also exposed the full extent of the damage inflicted upon Emily's life. The realization that her tormentor's actions were driven by personal pain rather than a direct vendetta against her did little to mitigate her own suffering. Instead, it compounded her sense of betrayal and despair.

The revelations about the hater's troubled past and their motives had leaked to the public, further intensifying the scrutiny and judgment Emily faced. The community's response was swift and harsh. Emily, once the center of attention and admiration, was now subjected to an onslaught of criticism and condemnation.

The school, which had initially rallied around her during the height of her popularity, was now a hostile environment. Rumours swirled, and whispers of scandal followed her wherever she went.

The students who had once been her friends were now distancing themselves, their support eroding as the full extent of the drama unfolded.

Emily's social media presence, which had been a source of both pride and stress, was now a battleground of negativity. The once-admiring followers who had celebrated her rise to fame were now quick to turn on her, fuelled by a mixture of outrage and schadenfreude. The online harassment was relentless, with people scrutinizing her every move and amplifying her mistakes.

Her parents, too, were caught in the crossfire. They faced judgment from friends, neighbour's, and even other parents who questioned their ability to protect their daughter from the fallout. The support they had once received had dwindled, replaced by a palpable sense of disapproval and blame.

Emily's once-close relationships with her friends had disintegrated. The fallout from the hater's actions had created a rift between her and those she had once considered her closest allies. The betrayal of the hater had not only shattered her public image but had also deeply impacted her personal connections.

In the midst of this turmoil, Emily struggled to find a sense of stability. The weight of her actions and the consequences they had wrought felt insurmountable. She was haunted by the knowledge that the hater's manipulations had not only destroyed her reputation but had also irrevocably altered the course of her life.

The consequences of the revelations were not limited to the external pressures Emily faced. Internally, she grappled with feelings of guilt and regret. The awareness of how her own actions had contributed to the chaos weighed heavily on her conscience. The realization that her pursuit of popularity and the mistakes she had made had led to such devastating outcomes was a harsh and painful truth to confront.

Emily's therapist, who had been a constant source of support throughout her ordeal, helped her navigate these complex emotions. Through therapy, Emily began to process her feelings of guilt and learn how to cope with the harsh realities of her situation. It was a slow and challenging process, but it was essential for her emotional healing.

The impact of the revelations extended beyond Emily's personal life. The community's reaction highlighted a broader issue of how social media and public scrutiny can magnify and distort individual experiences. The intense focus on Emily's story served as a stark reminder of the dangers of online bullying and the need for greater empathy and understanding in the digital age.

Emily's struggle to reconcile the truth with her own sense of self was a central theme in her ongoing journey. She faced the daunting task of rebuilding her life and finding a way to move forward despite the profound setbacks she had endured. The path to recovery was fraught with obstacles, but it was a necessary step toward regaining control and finding a sense of peace.

The haunting truth about the hater's motivations had revealed the complexities of human behaviour and the impact of unresolved personal issues on others. For Emily, the consequences of this revelation were both deeply personal and widely public. As she grappled with the fallout from the truth, she was forced to confront the full scope of the damage and work towards a future where she could find healing and redemption.

Chapter 11: The Unforgiving World

The days following the revelations about the hater were a whirlwind of condemnation and scrutiny for Emily. What had once been a thrilling ride of viral fame and high school popularity had now spiraled into a nightmare of public judgment and relentless hostility.

As the news about the hater's motivations spread, Emily became the focal point of a media frenzy. News outlets seized the opportunity to sensationalize her story, framing her as both a victim and a villain. Headlines screamed of her fall from grace, painting her in a light that only added to the swirling storm of negativity surrounding her. The media's portrayal of Emily was often harsh, with little regard for the nuances of her situation or the mental toll it was taking on her.

At school, the atmosphere had shifted drastically. The once supportive environment was now cold and judgmental. Emily's classmates, who had once admired her or at least been indifferent, now viewed her with disdain. Rumors spread like wildfire, each iteration more exaggerated and cruel than the last. Where there had been friendly faces and camaraderie, there was now a sea of hostile glares and whispered insults.

The social dynamics of the school had changed overnight. Emily's former friends, those who had once been by her side, now distanced themselves from her. The rift between Emily and her friends had been exacerbated by the hater's actions, and now, with the full story out in the open, many of them chose to sever ties. The sense of betrayal Emily felt was compounded by the realization that those who had once claimed to understand and support her were now abandoning her in her time of need.

Online, the situation was no better. Emily's social media accounts, once bustling with positive engagement, were now inundated with hateful comments and messages. The virtual platforms that had been a source of validation and connection had become a battleground of negativity. The cyberbullying was relentless, with anonymous users hurling insults and threats, fueling Emily's sense of isolation and despair.

The public backlash was not limited to Emily's peers and the media. The broader community weighed in with their judgments and opinions. Neighbors and local residents who had once welcomed her family with open arms now looked upon them with suspicion and disapproval. The small town of Willow Creek, which had initially seemed like a safe haven, had become a place of hostility and alienation.

Emily's parents were deeply affected by the public reaction. They had always been her biggest supporters, but the intense scrutiny and criticism they faced from the community took a toll on them. The stress of defending their daughter and dealing with the backlash was overwhelming, straining their relationship and adding to the family's collective sense of turmoil.

Despite their efforts to support her, Emily's parents struggled to shield her from the worst of the public reaction. The emotional strain on the family was palpable, and the once close-knit unit began to fray under the pressure. The walls of their home, which had once been a refuge, now felt like a prison, trapping them in a cycle of fear and anxiety.

The school administration, while sympathetic to Emily's situation, was also caught in a difficult position. They faced pressure from parents and students alike to address the fallout from the scandal. In an attempt to manage the situation, the school implemented measures to address bullying and harassment, but these actions often felt insufficient and poorly received.

Emily's struggle to navigate the harsh reality of public backlash was compounded by her own internal turmoil. She grappled with feelings of shame and guilt, questioning her own actions and their impact on those around her. The weight of the public's judgment and the disintegration of her social life created a sense of despair that was difficult to overcome.

In therapy, Emily worked to process the overwhelming emotions and cope with the harsh realities of her situation. Her therapist helped her to understand the importance of self-compassion and resilience in the face of adversity. The therapy sessions became a crucial outlet for Emily to express her feelings and develop strategies for managing the emotional and psychological impact of the backlash.

The fallout from the revelations was a stark reminder of the unforgiving nature of the public sphere and the challenges of dealing with a high-profile crisis. For Emily, the public backlash was not just an external obstacle but also a profound personal trial. It tested her ability to cope with the consequences of her actions and the relentless scrutiny that accompanied them.

As Emily faced the harsh realities of her situation, she was forced to confront the painful truth that her journey from viral fame to public disgrace had irrevocably altered her life. The public's unforgiving response served as a constant reminder of the fragility of reputation and the often harsh consequences of fame.

Emily's world felt like it was collapsing in on itself. The walls of her bedroom, once a refuge, now seemed to close in with every passing hour. The judgment and hostility from the community had reached an unbearable crescendo, and Emily was left grappling with the harsh reality of her situation. The public backlash had not only stripped her of her social standing but also isolated her from everyone she once trusted.

The media's portrayal of Emily as both a victim and a perpetrator had fueled a firestorm of negativity. The public's appetite for sensationalism had turned her story into a relentless spectacle. Online forums and social media platforms were awash with debates, insults, and misinformation. The opinions of anonymous strangers had become a constant presence in Emily's life, amplifying her sense of helplessness.

At school, the atmosphere was suffused with an unspoken but palpable hostility. The students who had once admired her now viewed her with disdain. The whispers in the hallways, the snide remarks, and the glaring stares all served as constant reminders of her fall from grace. The once-familiar environment of Willow Creek High had transformed into a battleground of social rejection and scorn.

Emily's former friends, those who had once been her support system, were now distant. The rift caused by the hater's machinations had widened, and the fracture lines in her relationships had become permanent. The emotional support she had hoped for from her closest peers was now absent, replaced by avoidance and, in some cases, outright hostility.

As she tried to navigate this treacherous landscape, Emily found herself at a crossroads. The weight of the public scrutiny and the collapse of her social support system had pushed her to a breaking point. She was faced with a critical decision: whether to fight back against the relentless barrage of negativity or to retreat entirely from the public eye.

The option to fight back was fraught with risks. Emily had already attempted to confront the situation head-on, but her efforts had often backfired, resulting in more public humiliation and exacerbating her sense of vulnerability. She was well aware that any further attempts to defend herself could be met with even harsher reactions, potentially worsening her situation.

On the other hand, disappearing entirely from the public sphere seemed like an appealing escape. The thought of deleting her social media accounts, abandoning her online presence, and withdrawing from school was increasingly tempting. The idea of retreating into anonymity and seeking solace in the privacy of her own space offered a brief respite from the constant bombardment of judgment.

Emily's internal struggle was intense and multifaceted. The pressure to make a decision was compounded by the fear of making the wrong choice. The decision to fight back might lead to further alienation and escalation, while the decision to disappear could be perceived as admitting defeat. The weight of these conflicting possibilities was overwhelming, leaving Emily paralyzed with indecision.

Her parents, though supportive, were themselves struggling to cope with the situation. They were caught between their desire to protect Emily and their own frustration at being unable to shield her from the public backlash. Their attempts to offer guidance were often met with Emily's resistance, as she grappled with feelings of guilt and shame over the turmoil she had caused.

In therapy, Emily's sessions became increasingly focused on exploring her feelings of despair and indecision. Her therapist encouraged her to consider the long-term implications of her choices and to evaluate the potential consequences of both fighting back and retreating. The therapeutic process aimed to help Emily regain a sense of agency and control over her own life, despite the external chaos.

Emily's friends, who had once been a source of comfort, were now absent from her life. The emotional isolation she felt was exacerbated by the absence of their support. The sense of betrayal and abandonment weighed heavily on her, adding to the already complex emotional landscape she was navigating.

As the pressure mounted, Emily found herself considering the possibility of a drastic move. The idea of attempting to expose the full truth behind the hater's motivations in a last-ditch effort to redeem herself was appealing, but also fraught with risk. The thought of revealing the full story, hoping it would somehow shift public opinion, was both a desperate and a courageous choice.

Emily's decision-making process was further complicated by the constant barrage of negative feedback she received. The online and offline bullying was relentless, leaving her feeling as though she was under constant surveillance and judgment. The emotional toll of the public backlash made it difficult for Emily to think clearly about her options and the potential consequences.

As the days went by, Emily's mental and emotional state continued to deteriorate. The decision she faced was not just about choosing between fighting back or retreating; it was also about confronting her own fears and vulnerabilities. The relentless negativity had taken a toll on her self-esteem and sense of self-worth, making it increasingly difficult for her to envision a path forward.

In the end, Emily was forced to confront the harsh reality of her situation. The public's unforgiving reaction had created a chasm between her and the world she once knew. Her former friends, the community, and the media had all contributed to a sense of isolation and despair that felt insurmountable.

Emily's final decision was a reflection of her internal turmoil and the external pressures she faced. The choice to fight back or disappear was not just about the immediate consequences but also about the long-term impact on her sense of self and her future. The weight of this decision was a heavy burden, and Emily's struggle to find clarity in the midst of overwhelming adversity was a testament to the profound challenges she faced.

Chapter 12: The Twisted Ending

Emily sat in her dimly lit room, the heavy curtains drawn against the outside world. The room was cluttered with remnants of her once vibrant online persona—merchandise, posters, and framed photos of happier times. Now, each item felt like a relic from a different life, a stark reminder of the whirlwind that had unraveled her existence.

The truth behind the hater's identity had been exposed, but the public's reaction had been overwhelmingly negative. The revelations had done little to shift the tide of hatred against Emily. Instead, they seemed to solidify the community's disdain, amplifying the sense of betrayal and disillusionment that surrounded her. The truth, once so tantalizing, had become another source of pain, a bitter pill that only added to her misery.

Emily's decision to make a final stand was born out of a desperate need for redemption, a desire to salvage something from the wreckage of her life. She believed that by exposing the full truth about the hater and their motivations, she might somehow clear her name or, at the very least, find some semblance of closure.

She began by drafting a detailed account of everything she had uncovered—emails, messages, screenshots, and personal testimonies. Her aim was to create a comprehensive narrative that would lay bare the extent of the hater's manipulations and the real reasons behind their relentless campaign against her. It was a meticulous process, fraught with the same anxiety and fear that had plagued her for months.

As she compiled the evidence, Emily grappled with a mix of hope and skepticism. She knew that this final attempt to set the record straight might not yield the results she hoped for. The damage had been done, and the public's perception of her had been irrevocably altered. Nonetheless, she pressed on, driven by the belief that she owed it to herself to fight for the truth.

The culmination of her efforts was a lengthy, detailed exposé that she posted on a new blog she had created anonymously. She used this platform to present her case, hoping that by removing her personal identity from the equation, she might avoid further backlash. The post was thorough, covering the timeline of events, the evidence she had collected, and the emotional toll it had taken on her.

Emily's blog post was accompanied by a video in which she spoke directly to the camera, her voice trembling with a mixture of fear and determination. In the video, she narrated the story behind the hater's actions, explaining how their own unresolved issues and personal vendettas had driven them to target her. It was a raw and emotional account, delivered with a vulnerability that was both heartbreaking and compelling.

As she hit "publish" on both the blog post and the video, Emily felt a fleeting sense of relief. She had done everything she could to set the record straight, and now, the outcome was beyond her control. The waiting period that followed was agonizing, filled with uncertainty about how the public and her former friends would respond.

In the days that followed, Emily's blog post garnered some attention, but the reaction was far from the vindication she had hoped for. The comments were a mix of support and criticism, with many readers expressing sympathy but others condemning her for not handling the situation differently. The public's reaction was polarized, and the overwhelming negativity continued to overshadow any potential for redemption.

Emily's attempts to reach out to her former friends were met with silence or curt responses. The damage to her relationships was profound, and the rift seemed insurmountable. The very people who had once been her support system now avoided her, their absence a constant reminder of her isolation.

Her parents, despite their best efforts, were unable to shield her from the ongoing fallout. They remained supportive, but their own frustration and helplessness were palpable. They had hoped that Emily's final attempt to expose the truth would bring some resolution, but it had only added to the complexity of the situation.

In the midst of this turmoil, Emily found herself grappling with the realization that her last-ditch effort to clear her name had been too little, too late. The public's perception of her had hardened, and the consequences of the hater's campaign were deeply entrenched in the fabric of her life. The finality of this realization left her feeling more desolate than ever.

Emily's mental state continued to deteriorate as she faced the harsh reality of her situation. The emotional weight of her failed attempt to reclaim her life, coupled with the ongoing public scrutiny, pushed her to the brink of despair. The sense of hopelessness that had been building over the months now felt overwhelming.

In her darkest moments, Emily questioned whether her efforts had made any difference at all. The idea of continuing to fight seemed increasingly futile, and the thought of disappearing from the public eye became more appealing. The pressure to maintain a facade of strength was exhausting, and the thought of escaping from the relentless negativity was a constant temptation.

The final attempt to expose the truth had not provided the redemption Emily had hoped for. Instead, it had underscored the depth of the damage that had been inflicted upon her life. As she came to terms with the consequences of her actions and the hater's relentless campaign, Emily found herself in a state of profound reflection and uncertainty.

The chapter of Emily's life that had once been filled with promise and potential had been irrevocably altered. The path she had taken to seek redemption had not led to the resolution she desired, and the journey had left her grappling with the harsh realities of her situation. The final stand she had taken was a poignant reminder of the complex interplay between truth, perception, and the consequences of public actions.

The aftermath of Emily's final stand was a cacophony of disillusionment and despair. Her last attempt to clear her name had not provided the catharsis she had desperately sought. Instead, it had intensified the scrutiny and vitriol directed at her. The community's reaction was a painful reminder of the unforgiving nature of public opinion, and Emily was left grappling with the harsh reality of her situation.

Emily's room, once a sanctuary, now felt like a prison. The walls, lined with posters of influencers and social media icons, seemed to close in on her. The remnants of her former life—a glittering world of online fame and friendship—now felt like a cruel joke. The photographs of smiling faces and celebratory moments were stark contrasts to the darkness that enveloped her now.

The flood of comments and messages following her last blog post was a mixture of pity, condemnation, and indifference. The sympathetic voices were drowned out by the overwhelming tide of negativity. The anonymous posts, taunts, and aggressive comments filled her inbox, each one a reminder of how far she had fallen from grace.

The weight of her isolation was crushing. The friends she had once relied on had distanced themselves, either out of fear of association or because they had simply moved on. The school hallways, once a place of tentative friendship and camaraderie, now felt alien and hostile. Her presence, once celebrated, was now met with whispers and sidelong glances.

Emily's family struggled to understand the extent of her pain. They tried to offer support, but their well-meaning efforts often felt inadequate in the face of her profound despair. Their concern was palpable, but their inability to fully grasp the scale of Emily's suffering left them feeling powerless.

Her parents' attempts to provide a semblance of normalcy—family dinners, conversations about school, and weekend outings—seemed futile. Emily's mind was consumed by a constant replay of her downfall, the relentless pressure, and the betrayal she had faced. She became increasingly withdrawn, preferring to spend her days alone in her room, lost in a spiral of self-loathing and regret.

As the days turned into weeks, Emily's mental and emotional state deteriorated further. The stress and anxiety that had once been manageable now felt overwhelming. The constant barrage of negative feedback and the lack of genuine support led her into a deepening depression. Her grades plummeted, and her once-vibrant social media presence was reduced to a desolate wasteland of forgotten posts and unanswered messages.

In her darkest moments, Emily contemplated the possibility of escape. The idea of disappearing from the public eye entirely became more appealing. The thought of severing all ties, deleting her online presence, and retreating into anonymity seemed like a way to reclaim some control over her shattered life. But even as she entertained these thoughts, a gnawing sense of futility lingered.

Emily's attempts to reach out for help were half-hearted. She attended a few therapy sessions but found it difficult to open up about the depth of her despair. The sessions often felt superficial, a temporary balm that did little to address the root of her anguish. Her reluctance to fully engage in the healing process was a barrier she struggled to overcome.

The turning point came when Emily received an anonymous message that pushed her over the edge. The message, laden with vitriol and threats, seemed to encapsulate everything she had been trying to escape. It was a final, cruel reminder of the relentless hatred that had plagued her. The message was a stark representation of the torment she had endured and the despair she felt.

The weight of this final insult was more than Emily could bear. The message became the catalyst for a series of desperate and self-destructive actions. Her sense of hopelessness reached a crescendo, and she found herself unable to envision a future beyond the torment she had endured. The idea of continuing to fight felt like an exercise in futility, and the thought of disappearing from everyone's view seemed like the only viable option.

Emily's final decision was made in the solitude of her room. She wrote a heartfelt letter, expressing her apologies and regrets, and then took a series of actions that left her family and friends in shock. The letter was a poignant testament to her inner turmoil and a final attempt to communicate her feelings to those she had left behind.

The fallout from Emily's final actions was profound. Her family was left grappling with a sense of disbelief and profound sorrow. The community, though initially shocked, quickly moved on, their attention shifting to the next sensational story. Emily's life, once filled with promise and potential, had become a cautionary tale—a haunting reminder of the destructive power of online fame and the unforgiving nature of public opinion.

The book closes on a somber note, with Emily's fate left unresolved and her story a poignant reflection on the complexities of modern life and the dangers of social media. The finality of her actions and the enduring sense of doom leave readers with a haunting impression, a reminder of the fragility of human emotions and the devastating impact of a relentless pursuit of validation.

The ending serves as a stark reflection on the consequences of a world driven by digital fame and the toll it can take on those who become ensnared in its web. Emily's story is a tragic exploration of the intersection between public perception and personal suffering, leaving readers with a lingering sense of melancholy and introspection.

Don't miss out!

Visit the website below and you can sign up to receive emails whenever Michael Ferguson publishes a new book. There's no charge and no obligation.

https://books2read.com/r/B-A-CKNW-FYQOE

BOOKS2READ

Connecting independent readers to independent writers.

Did you love *The Twisted Ending*? Then you should read *Obsessed With Shadows*[1] by Michael Ferguson!

[2]

In the sleepy town of Crestwood, 17-year-old Jake Marshall is an average high school senior with a passion for true crime podcasts and mystery novels. His quiet life takes a dramatic turn when the body of Lily Thompson, a popular and seemingly perfect classmate, is discovered in the nearby woods. The town is thrown into shock, and the investigation into Lily's death quickly becomes the talk of the community.

Intrigued and driven by his fascination with crime, Jake begins to delve into the case on his own. What starts as a mere curiosity

---

1. https://books2read.com/u/mZWRKl

2. https://books2read.com/u/mZWRKl

soon turns into an all-consuming obsession. As Jake digs deeper, he uncovers a series of unsettling truths about Lily's life that nobody else seems to know. He discovers that Lily was entangled in a complex web of relationships and secrets that reveal her life was far more complicated than her public persona suggested.

Jake's investigation leads him to receive anonymous threats, and he begins to notice that people around him are acting strangely. His friendships start to deteriorate, his academic performance suffers, and his once-stable life begins to unravel. The deeper Jake gets into the case, the more dangerous it becomes, as he realizes that someone is watching him and manipulating events to their advantage.

The investigation brings Jake face-to-face with unexpected allies and potential suspects. He uncovers hidden motives and dark agendas, all while struggling to maintain his own sanity. As he gets closer to the truth, the lines between reality and obsession blur, leading him into a dangerous game where he's not sure who he can trust.

In a shocking climax, Jake learns that the true mastermind behind the murder has been manipulating him all along, setting him up as the perfect scapegoat. He is faced with an impossible choice: to clear his name, he must commit a crime that would make him the very monster he's been hunting. The book concludes with Jake reflecting on the cost of his obsession and whether he can find a way to rebuild his life and seek redemption.

Obsessed with Shadows is a gripping and intense mystery that explores the fine line between passion and obsession, the consequences of pursuing the truth, and the impact of uncovering dark secrets. It takes readers on a thrilling journey through suspense and intrigue, challenging them to consider how far one might go in the quest for answers.

www.ingramcontent.com/pod-product-compliance
Lightning Source LLC
Chambersburg PA
CBHW071458130726
47997CB00006B/2395